MW00898959

Tales of the Sonoran Desert

Joyce Story

Copyright 2014 ©Joyce Story

Tales of the Sonoran Desert

All rights reserved. No part of this book may be reproduced or used without express permission by the author except in brief quotations for the purpose of review or critical analysis.

ISBN: 978-1494228125

Printed in the USA

Illustrations by Audrey Lee
http://AllOfMe.me

Publishing Services
DMBookPro.com

PRAISE FOR
TALES OF THE SONORAN DESERT

These lovely tales show us the beauty of the Sonoran Desert and all its inhabitants - plant and animal! - and gently teach us lessons that we share with all living things.
Marcia Wade, M.A.T.

For many people folktales are something old and quaint, encompassing European fairy tales and early American folklore. But stories are still being told--from urban myths to tales around the campfire. While some of us may occasionally wonder "what if walls could talk," Joyce Story gives voice to a variety of southwestern flora and fauna. And what tales they tell. This book should appeal to those who love animals, deserts, and good stories.
Elizabeth Hufford, M.A.

The Abrahamic religions---Christianity, Judaism and Islam---affirm that, though life began in the Garden, faith was born in the desert. Moses, Jesus and Mohammed were all shaped by experiences in wilderness. Though the Sonoran Desert has much to teach us, many of those lessons can be harsh. If we aren't careful, the land without water can kill us. Joyce Story mediates the teachings of the desert with wit and wisdom. Like Aesop, she creates fables where animals find their voice, and we can listen and learn. Open up her stories and come on in. The desert is fine!
Rev. Doug Bland, M.Div.

Introduction

The Sonoran Desert is quite unusual as far as deserts go. Because of the remarkable variety of its vegetative growth, which shows the greatest diversity of any desert on earth, the Sonoran Desert is even called "lush." It has an impressive number of animal species as well: for starters, there are more than 1000 different kinds of native bees and 350 species of birds.

One of four deserts in North America, the Sonoran Desert covers some 100,000 square miles. It is located both in Mexico, where it spans half the state of Sonora and nearly the entire Baja California peninsula, and in the United States, where it stretches across southeasternmost California and the western and central parts of southern Arizona.

Located in the Sonoran Desert of Arizona is the city of Phoenix, the state capital and the seat of Maricopa County. The latter boasts ten regional parks, all of which are dedicated to preserving the desert while offering opportunities for the public to understand and personally experience this unique and beautiful land. As a storyteller, I have regularly shared my *Tales of the Sonoran Desert* at one of them, the White Tank Mountain Regional Park. To Raymond Schell, Park Supervisor, I extend my sincere gratitude for his unfailing and gracious support.

CONTENTS

Part One: Ways in the Wilderness

Part Two: Weavings in the Wilderness

Part One

Ways in the Wilderness

The desert is commonly seen as a land where one faces the ultimate test of survival.

The following stories about the plants and animals of the Sonoran Desert are united by this challenge of finding a way through the wilderness.

The Secret of Dreaming

*The creation story that follows is an adaptation of a work
entitled "The Secret of Dreaming" by Jim Poulter, an Australian
writer well versed in Aboriginal mythology.*

*Set in the Sonoran Desert, the version offered below begins with
animals of the Sea of Cortez, the body of water that essentially
cuts the Mexican portion of the desert in half.*

Once there was nothing, nothing but the Spirit of All Life.
For a long time, there was nothing.
Then, in the Mind of the Spirit of Life,
a Dreaming began.

In the empty darkness there was a Dreaming of Fire,
and the color of Fire burned brightly in the Mind of the Great
Spirit.
Then came a Dreaming of Wind,
and the Fire danced and swirled in the Mind of the Spirit of
Life.
Next there was a Dreaming of Rain.
For a long time, Fire, Wind, and Rain raged in the Dreaming.
Then, as their fury diminished,
there came a Dreaming of Earth and Sky and of Land and Sea.

For a long time this Dreaming continued.

Then the Great Spirit sent Life into the dream
so that Creator Spirits could continue the Dreaming
and the dream would be real.

The Spirit of Life sent the Secret of Dreaming
into the world with the Spirit of the Striped Marlin.
The Marlin entered the deep, still waters
...and began to dream.
It dreamed of waves and wet sand
but without understanding them.
It wanted to dream only of deep, still water.

The Marlin passed the Secret of Dreaming
on to the Spirit of the Sea Turtle.
The Turtle came out of the waves onto the wet sand
...and began to dream.

It dreamed of rocks and warm sun
but did not understand them.
It wanted to dream only of waves and wet sand.

The Turtle passed the Secret of Dreaming
on to the Spirit of the Leopard Lizard.
The Lizard climbed onto a rock, felt the warm sun on its back,
...and began to dream.
It dreamed of the wind and the open sky
but without understanding them.
It wanted to dream only of rocks and warm sun.

The Lizard passed the Secret of Dreaming
on to the Spirit of the Golden Eagle.
The Eagle rose up into the open sky, felt the wind in its wings,
...and began to dream.
It dreamed of trees and night sky
but did not understand them.
It wanted to dream only of wind and open sky.

The Eagle passed the Secret of Dreaming
on to the Spirit of the Ringtail.
The Ringtail climbed high into a tree, looked at the night sky,
...and began to dream.
It dreamed of cactus, shrubs, and grasses
but without understanding them.
It wanted to dream only of trees and of night sky.

The Ringtail passed the Secret of Dreaming
on to the Spirit of the Pronghorn.
The Pronghorn raced among the cactus, shrubs, and grasses
...and began to dream.
It dreamed of song and dance and laughter,
but it did not understand them.
It wanted to dream only of shrubs and grasses.

The Pronghorn passed the Secret of Dreaming
on to the Spirit of Woman and Man.
Together Woman and Man walked across the land.
They saw all the works of creation,
all the things that had been dreamed before:

    the deep, still waters,
    the waves and wet sand,

the rocks and open sky,
the trees and night sky,
and the bushes and grassy expanses.

And they began to dream ...

They dreamed of sharing
the morning music of the Curved Bill Thrasher,
the daytime dance of the Longfin Dace,
and the jubilant roar of the Jaguar at the setting of the saffron sun.

Woman and Man realized
that every Creature
was their Spirit Cousin
whose Dreaming they must protect.

Then they dreamed of the laughter of Children.
Woman and Man understood that dream.
They dreamed of how they would tell all these secrets
to their Child who was not yet born.

Knowing, at last, that the Secret of Dreaming
was safe with Woman and Man,
the Spirit of Life entered the Land to rest.

Now, when the Spirits of all Creatures have grown weary,
they join the Spirit of Life in the Land.

That is why the Land is sacred,
and why it is we
who must safeguard and nurture it.

THE DESERT TORTOISE AND
THE FREE-TAILED BAT

Even when success seems impossible, there may be a way to prevail.

Long ago in the Sonoran Desert, a Mexican free-tailed bat was winging about above a desert wash. Then, as now, this bat could fly very fast—up to 60 mph—and it could fly higher than any other bat. Its flying abilities, along with the fact that its thin tail extended farther than that of most other bats, led the Mexican free-tailed bat to be quite taken with itself. "Look how my tail whips around in the air as I fly up so high and with such speed. I am something else!"

As the bat whooshed down close to the wash, it noticed a desert tortoise, slowly climbing up a dirt ramp on the side of the wash.

"Sheesh," said the bat. "You're so slow! And you can barely lift yourself up off the ground! And you don't even have a tail!"

"In fact, I do have a tail," the tortoise replied, "a nice fat one, curled up under my shell."

"Well, look how you're lumbering along, and you're stuck on the ground, to boot. It's pitiful! Not like me—ah, the views I have when I fly way up in the air. And I'm so fast that nothing can get away from me!"

"You know," said the tortoise, "perhaps there are things that you don't see because you fly so high and so fast. After all, you didn't see my nice fat tail. I don't think that there is any reason to feel sorry for me. I can move as fast as I need to."

"But not fast enough to outrace me!" said the bat.

"I'm willing to race you. We can make a bet. Whoever loses will have to admit that the winner is truly a superior being."

So it was that the desert tortoise challenged the Mexican free-tailed bat to a race. The bat laughed out loud—the very idea! But it agreed to meet the tortoise the next morning at the same spot, and the two would race to the end of the wash.

That night the tortoise called together all its family. "I'm going to be in a race with the free-tailed bat," it said.

"Are you crazy?" all of them asked in astonishment.

"Well, I have a plan," the tortoise answered.

The next morning the bat flew to the starting line, where the tortoise was already waiting. On the count of three, the race began.

The tortoise began plodding along. The bat darted up into the sky and flew in fast loops above the desert wash. After a while, it decided to go to the first stopping point on the race track, a large tank, or depression, in the rock that was filled with water. Thirsty from all its effort, the bat was glad to swoop down to lap up some water. It wasn't glad, however, to see that the tortoise was already there, calmly drinking its fill.

"I must have made a few too many loops," thought the bat. "I'll have to stay more on course."

The two set off again. This time the bat made fewer loops. Nonetheless, it was still sure that it would have no problem staying ahead of the tortoise, so it flew as high as it could up into the sky. Off to one side, it saw a cloud of moths, one of its favorite dishes. The bat dashed over to the moths and—*slurp*—ate them all! Now it flew straight to the second stopping point in the race, that is, the ephedra bush, also known as the Mormon tea bush.

Who was already there? It was the tortoise, sipping a cup of Mormon tea.

"Where have you been?" the tortoise asked. "I was worried about you. Here, have some tea; you look like you could use a pick-me-up."

"I don't believe it!" thought the bat. "This time, I'm flying straight to the finish line. That pokey tortoise can't possibly get there before I do."

However, when the bat arrived at the finish line, huffing and puffing from all its haste, there was the tortoise, singing a tortoise tune. To you and me it would have sounded like hissing and popping sounds and wouldn't have made any sense. But the bat understood it. The gist of the song was:

Hello, mister uppity bat,
How are you today?
Not so good and not so fast
As the tortoise, I dare say!

The Mexican free-tailed bat was so ashamed that it had lost the race to the desert tortoise—*puh-leeze*—that it flew right back to its cave and wouldn't come out except at night, when most of the animals were asleep. Even now it comes out only at night.

As for the desert tortoise, it immediately sent out messages of thanks to its family. You see, there were four tortoises involved in that race with the bat. One was stationed at the starting line; a second was waiting at the tank; a third had tea ready at the ephedra bush; and the fourth was ready to sing at the finish line.

Today the desert tortoise is a protected species, and we certainly want to make every effort to protect it. What if it became involved in a race with some other high-speed animals? It would need all its family to help!

THE PHAINOPEPLA AND THE DESERT MISTLETOE

A plant and an animal of the Sonoran Desert develop a
relationship that ensures their mutual survival.

Long ago, a new bird came to the Sonoran Desert. It was a beautiful bird, with jet black feathers that glistened in the sunlight and a fancy, pointed crest on its head.

"Who are you?" asked the other birds.

"I'm a phainopepla," the new arrival answered.

"A phai-no-what?" The birds found it hard to wrap their beaks around the word "phainopepla." "Well, with that crest and all, you look like a cardinal to us, a black cardinal."

"You can call me a black cardinal if you want to, but my real name is phainopepla. It means 'shining robe.'"

Some of the birds practiced the name "phainopepla" until they were able to say it, and that was what they called the new arrival. Other birds found that name too hard to remember, and they settled on "black cardinal."

By whatever name it was called, however, the bird had been traveling a long time, and it was hungry. There were plenty of insects for it to eat, but it had to have something more than insects. Juicy berries were what it needed!

The phainopepla caught sight of the round, orange berries of the hackberry bush. It quickly flew over to the bush, already savoring the delicious looking fruit.

But the hackberry bush shook its branches at the phainopepla. "Shoo," said the plant. "Go away! I already feed a multitude of birds, and I don't need you hanging around."

The phainopepla was very disappointed, but then it saw the oval, orange-red berries of the wolfberry bush. They looked even more inviting than the hackberries. But it, too, would not allow the phainopepla to eat any of its fruit.

"I can't feed every Tom, Dick, and phai-, phai-, phai-," it said, stumbling on the new bird's name. It settled on the name 'Harry.'

The phainopepla was becoming worried. It really did need to eat some berries. Eating nothing but insects just wouldn't do. After all, bird does not live by bug alone!

"I'll share my berries with you," said a little voice that seemed to come from way down on the ground.

The phainopepla had to look all around before it finally spotted a plant growing at the very bottom of a mesquite tree. It was hard to see, but even if it had been easily seen, it wouldn't have attracted attention because there was nothing special about it. Most of the time it was just a stringy clump of brittle stems without any leaves. As a result, even when it produced its pink-red berries, the plant was largely ignored.

Growing as it did at the bottom of the mesquite tree, it had long ago become tired of seeing nothing but the ground around it and the mesquite's narrow leaves and light-yellow flowers. It longed to be up in the top of the tree and to make its home in other kinds of trees as well so that it could see more of the world around it. But there it was, stuck at the bottom of the mesquite tree, which, like it or not, played the role of host, for the shrub depended on the tree for water and some nutrients. It was a partial parasite, and it was called mesquite mistletoe.

And now, unlike the hackberry and the wolfberry bushes, the mesquite mistletoe was offering to share its fruit with the phainopepla.

"Why, thank you," said the phainopepla. "Don't mind if I do!" It gobbled up as many berries as it could.

"They're delicious," it said. "But, my, the seeds are sticky!"

The bird flew up to the top of the mesquite and to other trees such as the palo verde, the ironwood, and the acacia, and it wiped its bill on the branches of those trees to clean off the sticky seeds. The seeds stuck to the branches like glue! Of course, not all the seeds in the berries stuck to the phainopepla's bill. Many of them were swallowed and passed right through the bird's digestive system. When the phainopepla left droppings on the branches of the trees, the seeds stuck there, too.

This development was quite advantageous for the mistletoe, because its seeds did not need soil in order to grow; they could grow directly on the branches of the trees! In no time at all, there were clusters of mistletoe in so many places that the plant came to be called desert, as well as mesquite, mistletoe.

So it was that the phainopepla and the desert mistletoe developed a close friendship that lasts to this very day and that greatly benefits them both. The plant provides the bird with the berries that are one of the main sources of its food and one with the vitamins and minerals necessary for a healthy, heart-smart lifestyle. At the same time, the phainopepla enables the desert mistletoe to have multiple homes in which to raid its host's refrigerator and from which to view the fascinating world of the Sonoran Desert.

THE BIRDS PETITION THE CREATOR

It is wise to follow the way of humility.

When the world and its creatures first came into being, all the birds were exactly alike. Their feathers were a rich chocolate in color and were as shiny as satin. Their stout bills all came to a sharp point. The birds all had a three-foot wing span. Everything about them was just the same, and the birds were very pleased.

Then they looked around at the newly created world. Everywhere they saw so much diversity that the world seemed to be a riot of differences.

They considered the fish. They saw all sizes, all the colors of the rainbow, and never-ending patterns of design on the bodies of the fish. As one bird noted, moreover, "You can't see any teeth at all on the catfish, but the great white shark—it's nothing but teeth!"

"Hmm," said the birds.

The birds looked at the bears. The bears all had a healthy set of teeth, but they, too, differed in appearance. There were black bears, there were polar bears, which were white, and there were panda bears, which were both black and white.

"Hmmm," said the birds.

The birds turned their attention to the flowers. There were purple pansies that bobbed just barely off the ground. There were pink hollyhocks that stood as tall and as straight as sentries. There were bright yellow sunflowers that faced east in the morning and west in the afternoon.

"Hmmmm," said the birds.

They began to talk among themselves about appealing to the Creator to make some changes. "Well, it won't hurt to try," the birds decided, and off they went.

"Creator," they said, "please don't get us wrong. We think your world is just fine, and we truly think we're fine, too. But we all look alike, and we were wondering if maybe we could be different from each other like so many of the plants and animals are."

"Sure," the Creator said. "Just tell me what you want, and it will be so."

The birds were atwitter with excitement, and they all lined up to tell the Creator their wishes.

The first bird in line said, "Creator, I want my crown and my throat to be crimson red and to sparkle in the sun. And I want a very long bill."

"Fine," said the Creator. "You'll be the Anna's hummingbird." And so it was.

The hummingbird, very proud of its new appearance, flew up to the top of a tall rock to watch the rest of the proceedings.

"Creator," said the next bird, "please make my back and wings have black and white stripes. Black and white is such a sophisticated combination!"

"Very well," said the Creator. "You'll be the Gila woodpecker." And so it was.

The hummingbird looked down from its perch on the rock and said, "Good grief. Black and white stripes? You look like a jail bird!"

The Creator gave the hummingbird the kind of look that means "Careful, now!"

Then the Creator turned to the next bird in line. "Creator," said this third bird, "I like the idea of having something on the top of my head. How about a distinctive crest? And flying around is all well and good, but would you please give me a pair of strong legs and feet? I want to run and feel the ground beneath my feet!"

"Not a problem," said the Creator. "You'll be the roadrunner." And so it was.

The hummingbird looked down and just couldn't refrain from giving its opinion.

"If you want to know the truth, that crest looks like a mop, and your legs and feet are anything but graceful."

Again the Creator looked at the hummingbird. "You know, if you can't say something nice, don't say anything at all!"

The next bird in line spoke up. "Creator, what I want, on the top of my head, is a curved plume. Then I'll be like a little girl who has a little curl right in the middle of her forehead."

"All right," said the Creator. "You'll be the Gambel's quail."

The hummingbird could not resist voicing its thoughts.

"That thing on the top of your head looks like an incomplete question mark. It's as if you started asking a question and then half way through forgot what you were saying. It looks dumb!"

Well, that did it. In a flash the hummingbird found itself sitting in the cup of the Creator's hands. "You asked me for a long bill," said the Creator in a disappointed tone, "and I gave you one. The long tongue that goes with it is for drinking nectar, not for saying unkind things about others. No more of this!"

In spite of the Creator's gentleness, the hummingbird felt so mortified that it made itself as tiny as it could, and it remains small to this very day! As for the rest of the birds, the Creator worked with them until they had all been granted the changes they requested. The birds were amazingly imaginative in their appeals, and we can only stand in awe of the Creator's handiwork.

How the Mountain Lion
Met His Match

The disadvantaged find the courage
and the means to take a stand.

A long time ago, one of the animals of the Sonoran Desert became quite impressed with himself. It was the mountain lion. Actually, he wasn't a lion at all, he was a cougar, but he was called a mountain lion, and the name went to his head. He knew about the lions in Africa, you see, and he took his cue from them.

"I," he announced one day to the astonishment of the plants and the other animals, "am the King—the King of the Mountain. And you must treat me as the royal, magnificent being that I am."

The mountain lion then informed all the animals and the plants of a new rule.

"When I walk by," he said, "you will bow—all the way to the ground."

Although the animals found this new rule objectionable, they weren't overly concerned about it, because for the most part, when they saw the mountain lion coming, they could escape. The birds could fly away, the gophers could scurry into their holes, and the snakes could slither into the rocks.

The saguaro cactus and the tall trees thought of a way to get around this new rule. "If we bow down," they said, "we'll crush you with our weight."

"Quite right," said the mountain lion. "Instead of bowing down as I pass by, you can just call out, 'Hail, O mighty King of the Mountain!'"

The saguaro and the trees laughed to themselves. "Who does he think he is!"

"We have a better idea," they suggested. "When you pass by, we'll imitate bells ringing, and we'll sing out, 'Ding-a-ling! Ding-a-ling!'"

The mountain lion's opinion of himself knew no limits, but his vocabulary did, and he didn't know that "ding-a-ling" meant "idiot." So he had no idea that when the saguaro and the trees sang out, "Ding-a-ling," they were calling him a fool.

The other plants, however, had no recourse, so when the mountain lion strutted around, they would bow down. If a plant didn't bow fast enough or low enough, the mountain lion would snarl and hiss at it and would even stomp on it. He was big and strong and could cause a lot of injury, and the plants were afraid of him.

The time came, however, when one group of the chollas had had it. They held a council to discuss what they could do. They were in a rebellious mood, but how could they rebel? They were just plants, and rather puny ones at that. The branches at the top of their stems had only a few spines here and there that offered some protection from small animals. But what could they do to defend themselves against the mountain lion?

Some of the older chollas argued that having to bow to the mountain lion was indeed offensive, but it was easier and more prudent just to accept the situation and live their lives in peace. But the younger chollas were of a different mind.

"Oh, no," they said. "There must be some way we can fend off that egomaniac."

Finally, they had an idea. "Let's all grow more spines, as many as we can. But we'll keep them inside so they won't be noticeable. When the time is right, we can make good use of them."

The chollas continued to bow down when the mountain lion swaggered past them. He had no idea that they were secretly producing more spines. The time came when there was no more room inside their branches for storing those extra spines. D-Day had arrived!

The mountain lion came prancing down the path. He came closer and closer. Not a single cholla made a move to bow.

"What's with this lack of respect?" hissed the mountain lion. He came right up to the chollas, opened his large mouth, and snarled.

Still they did not bow.

The mountain lion backed off a few yards, got a running start, and leapt into the air, straight toward the chollas. When he was mid-air, he heard one of them shout out a battle command. It was "Bristle!"—the cholla equivalent of "Fire!" All the chollas thrust their spines straight out. There were so many spines that they completely covered the chollas' branches.

The mountain lion landed right on the chollas, and, oh, my, how those spines hurt! What's more, they wouldn't let go! The mountain lion limped off, moaning and groaning, and it was months before he got all those spines out.

After that, the mountain lion lost interest in being the King of the Mountain, and life went back to a more normal routine. The chollas liked their new appearance, however, and they decided to keep their many spines. They still have all those spines today. There are so many of them that they give the plants a soft, fuzzy look, and some people call them teddy bear chollas. But they aren't like teddy bears at all. They are like warriors wearing silvery green headdresses, always ready to defend themselves.

The mountain lion isn't the only one to keep his distance from the chollas. If we're smart, so do we!

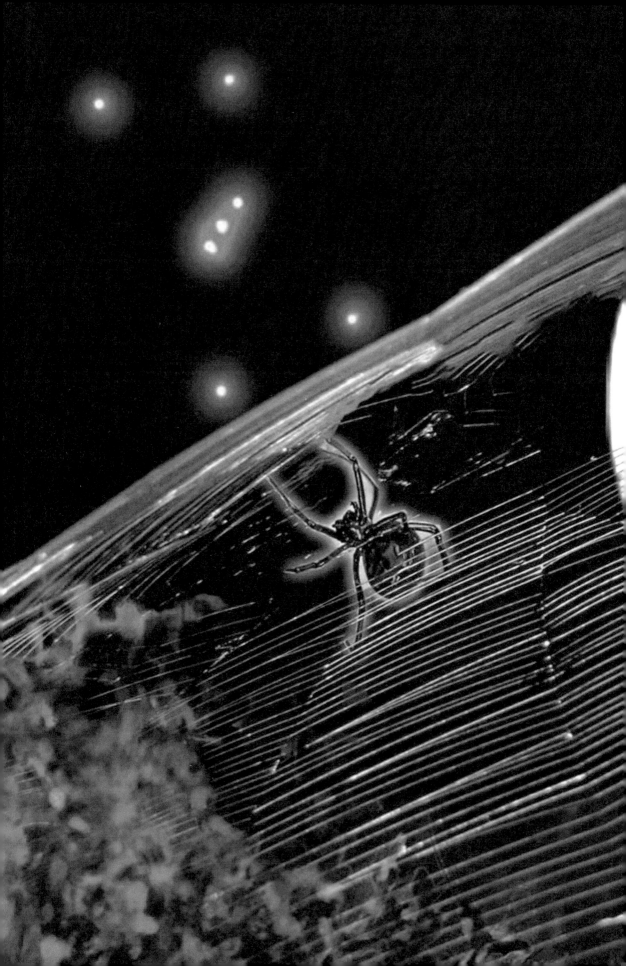

The Return of the Night Sky

Sometimes an unexpected partnership
can achieve what is needed.

Long ago, something very strange happened in the Sonoran Desert. First, the stars grew fainter and fainter, until they simply disappeared from the night sky. After a while, the moon ceased to go through the phases of a full moon, a half moon, and a crescent moon. Night after night, she was what we call the new moon, either not visible at all or, at best, a small sliver of light visible only in the early evening sky.

The animals that came out at night were especially affected by all this darkness. They had to have some light to make their way at night. Without any at all, it was hard for them to find food and to move about without bumping into something. They became dangerously thin and were always nursing injuries.

"This can't go on," they said. "We'll either starve to death or die from our wounds. And we animals aren't the only ones who are threatened. The saguaro, the queen of the night, and other night blooming plants won't survive, either; they need some light to produce healthy flowers."

The animals decided to consult with a certain bush in the desert—the creosote. Like today, the creosote bush could live for a very long time, more than a thousand years! If the animals were to find a way to deal with this problem, the solution would come from the creosote, which was very old and very wise. All the animals gathered around the bush to ask for its help.

"Ah," said the creosote. "I remember when there was a gleaming moon and sparkling stars in the night sky. But then the stars began growing dim. They weren't going out. What was happening was that the sky was being cloaked, or covered, and when the cover grew thick and hard enough, starlight could not shine through it. For a while the moon continued to go through her phases, but finally she grew so sad and lonely that she began to rise and set only when the sun did, so that she had some company. But then she couldn't be seen at night."

"Is there anything that can be done?" asked the animals.

"Here is what I advise," answered the bush. "Holes must be made in the cover so that the stars can shine through. When the moon realizes that the stars are back, she will resume the phases of her journey across the sky."

The animals knew that to make holes in the hard cover cloaking the sky, an animal had to have a sharp, pointed bill and very strong head and neck muscles. "I am the one for the job," said the Gila woodpecker. Everyone agreed. But how was the Gila woodpecker going to get all the way up to the sky? He certainly couldn't fly all the way up there.

The ants spoke up. "We can build a pyramid of sand up to the sky," they suggested.

"But that would take too long!" cried the rest of the animals.

"Oh, you don't know how many of us there are," replied the ants.

The animals turned to the creosote to settle the matter.

"It's true that there are a lot of you," the bush said to the ants. "But a strong wind could blow your work away, and even if that didn't happen, you'd have to use up all the sand in the desert to complete your project. Then nothing would survive!"

The ants had to agree that they were not the best choice to help the Gila woodpecker get up to the sky.

A small black spider spoke up. "The silk that I spin is very strong," she said, "and I can spin a web all the way to the sky. I'll go with the woodpecker."

The spider and the woodpecker began their work. First, the spider would weave her web higher and higher until she was too tired to spin any longer. She would rest while the woodpecker made his arduous flight to catch up with her. Then, while the bird rested, the spider would continue weaving her silken threads. Working in stages like this, they finally reached the sky.

The woodpecker set to work boring a hole in the sky. At last he pierced the cover, and the light of a star burst through the hole. It was a fiery hot light, and it burned the top of the woodpecker's head.

Their work was not finished. There had to be enough stars shining through to encourage all the rest to penetrate the cover blocking the sky. The spider wove her web in several directions, and the woodpecker bored six more holes in the cover over the sky.

The seven stars were delighted to see the world below again, and they lost no time in spreading the word. Soon all the stars followed their lead, fiercely burning through the cover and filling the night sky like glittering jewels. The moon realized that she would no longer be alone in the night sky, and she began to appear in her all her guises, from crescent-shaped to round and full.

Today the Gila woodpecker still has a red circle on the top of his head; it is the mark of the starfire that burned him when he made that first hole in the sky. The black spider has a red mark now also, on her abdomen. Some people say that it looks like an hour glass. Actually, the mark reflects what the ancient Greeks called the belt and the torso of the legendary hunter Orion. But when the plants and animals of the Sonoran desert look up and see that part of what is known today as the Orion constellation, they know that they are looking at the first seven stars that reappeared in the night sky, thanks to the Gila woodpecker and the black widow spider.

LARCENA PAGE AND THE BEYOND WORLD

In March of 1860, a young married couple named Larcena and John Page went to the mouth of Madera Canyon in the Santa Rita Mountains, near Tucson, Arizona. There they set up a small camp, close to the logging camp where John was employed. With them was a ten or eleven-year-old Mexican girl, Mercedes Sais Quiroz, whom Larcena was tutoring in English.

One morning, when Larcena and Mercedes were alone in their camp, they were taken captive by five Tonto Apaches. The Apaches forced Larcena and Mercedes to move quickly with them up the mountain. Since Larcena was not in good health, it was difficult for her to keep up. After they had traveled about 15 miles, the Apaches grew impatient with the delays she was causing. They stripped her of her shoes and most of her clothing, and they pierced her repeatedly with their spears. Then they threw her over a ledge and left her for dead.

Some two weeks later she was discovered lying on a road near the logging camp. This story traces her incredible journey down the mountain.

When the critically wounded Larcena Page was thrown by her Apache captors over a ledge, she fell down into another world, one very different from ours. It was the Beyond World, the Spirit World, for Larcena was somewhere between the world of the living and that of the dead.

There was snow in the shadow under the tree where Larcena now lay, and the Spirit of the Snow spoke. "Perhaps, if it were still the time of winter," it said to the Spirit Tree, "I would take her. But now I will hold her in my embrace."

Enveloped by the snow, Larcena lay unconscious for the rest of the day. At twilight, she heard dogs barking and men, including her husband, calling her name. But they could not hear her, for Larcena was in the Beyond World.

Again she passed out and lay unconscious for two days. On the third day she awoke. She was cold and thirsty. The Spirit Snow gave up its water for her and then told her, "You must leave, Larcena. If you are to be saved, you must go down the mountain and return to your people."

The Spirit Tree spoke to her, too. "Your journey will be one of great pain," it said. "To succeed, you must remain strong and determined."

Barefooted and dressed only in a bloodstained chemise, Larcena began to stagger down the mountain among the rocks. The Spirit Rocks were not so kind as the Spirit Snow. They cut her feet and filled the cuts with stones. When Larcena could no longer walk and had to crawl, the Spirit Rocks scraped her knees and her hands almost to the bone.

The spiny and thorny Spirit Plants bristled at Larcena's intrusion, and they delighted in digging into her arms and legs.

The Spirit Sun was indifferent to Larcena, and she both suffered and benefitted from its indifference. During the day, as the Sun crossed the sky, it brutally burned her shoulders and her arms. But early in the morning, it was the Spirit Sun that provided the warmth she needed to stop shaking from the cold of the night and to move ahead.

For days, Larcena made her way down the mountain on her hands and knees, sometimes slipping and sliding and sometimes having to retrace her path in order to get around an impassable barrier.

For food, she ate edible grasses and wild onions. These Spirit Beings gladly offered themselves to her. "We're sorry that we are so sparse," they said to her. "We see that you are becoming weaker and weaker, and we wish we could give you more." Larcena ate what she could find and pulled herself on.

Once she chanced upon a large pile of dried brush and grass. It looked so inviting that she could not resist stopping to rest. She climbed up on the pile. It was soft, almost like a bed, and she wearily closed her eyes. Suddenly the Spirit Gopher came out from its burrow. "No, Larcena," it called out. "This is the home of my brother, the Spirit Bear. You cannot stay. Leave! Leave now!" Larcena continued on.

On about the twelfth day, Larcena clawed her way up over a high ridge. As she looked down, she saw, far away, the first traces of her world: some men and a team of oxen. But the men did not see her, for Larcena was in the Beyond World.

Larcena sank to the ground in exhaustion. But at that moment the Spirit Wren flew over her, encouraging her. "You're almost there, Larcena. Don't give up now."

Larcena struggled on, for two more days. Finally she came to the camp of the men whom she had seen from the ridge. She was now at the threshold between the two worlds—the Beyond World and the one she had left so many days before.

She revived a fire in the camp. She found some flour, mixed it with water from the creek, made some dough, and cooked it. When she ate this simple bread, she entered into the outer reaches of her world.

She dragged herself to the road where she knew the loggers had to pass.

Some say that it was the logging camp's cook who first saw her. He was a simple, uneducated man who viewed anything that appeared unnatural as something ominous, if not evil. As far as the cook knew, lying on the road before him was something inhuman, something skeletal thin with hair tangled and matted with blood, something wearing a dirty and tattered shroud.

Is it surprising that he was deeply frightened, that he saw the creature as a terrifying being from another world? After all, Larcena had come from the Beyond World.

The cook ran to the camp for a weapon, and several men, their curiosity aroused by his ravings, went back to the road with him. When Larcena heard their voices, she raised her head. With her last ounce of strength, she said, "I am Larcena Page."

With these words, her agonizing quest was over. Larcena had returned to her world and to salvation.

It took a long time, but Larcena recovered from her injuries and her weakened state. A ransom was later paid for Mercedes, and the child was returned unharmed.

Thereafter, whenever Larcena felt a soft breeze blowing on her face, she fancied that she could hear it whispering to her, "Well done, Larcena. Well done."

Part Two

Weavings in the Wilderness

The desert is often perceived as a place of solitude where, paradoxically, one must dwell in order to experience the interconnectedness of all life. The following stories about the plants and animals of the Sonoran Desert are united by this weaving of ties in the wilderness.

How the Ocotillo Saved a Baby

*Near the present-day city of Tucson, Arizona, stand the
Santa Rita Mountains. They are part of the phenomena
in the American Southwest known as Sky Islands, that is,
forested mountain ranges surrounded by seas of desert.*

*In this story, an act of compassion that scars the
one who performs it remains an act of beauty.*

Long ago, there was an ocotillo bush growing in the Sonoran
Desert close to the Santa Rita Mountains. When it rained,
small green leaves would cover the branches of the ocotillo.
At least, leaves were supposed to cover its branches. But since
many animals in the area looked upon those leaves as gourmet
delights, the ocotillo had to contend with numerous and
significantly large bald spots. The desert rains were rare, however,
so for most of the time, the ocotillo's branches didn't have any
leaves on them at all. That was when the bush was at its most
impressive, for its branches were like smooth glass and were a
bright turquoise in color. The ocotillo was a modest sort and would
never brag, though it did often think to itself, "My, my, the Creator
made a mighty fine choice when it came to the color of my
branches!"

Then one spring, there was a very late and severe storm up in
the mountains. The wind rushed down onto the valley floor more
fiercely than any wind the ocotillo had ever experienced. The
branches of the bush whipped about in the wind so violently that
the ocotillo was sure that they would all snap off. Finally, when
the wind died down and all the stirred-up dust settled, the ocotillo
realized that the storm had left in its wake various unusual things:
pine needles, a live coal, and two unknown visitors—one lying on
the ground just a few feet away, rolled up in a ball, and the other
perched on one of the ocotillo's branches.

The creature perched on the branch was extremely talkative.
"Well, I never," it said. "What a terrible storm! I thought that that
wind would never stop. And look at me—I'm covered with dust;

you can't even see how pretty my blue gray feathers are. Let me get all this dust off. Brr! It's cold! Now, let me see. Just where am I?"

The ocotillo interrupted all this chatter and activity. "Excuse me," it said, "but who are you?" It recognized the creature as a bird, but the ocotillo had never seen it before since it lived up in the mountains.

"I'm a Mexican jay," answered the bird.

Before the ocotillo could say anything in response, the bird looked down at the creature at the foot of the bush and exclaimed, "Look! It's a porcupine—and a newborn one at that! See, its spines are soft. You know, they won't harden for about an hour. Well, I'll be. That wind just picked both of us up and blew us down here. Now that baby porcupine needs its mother. It will die without her. Well, I can't stay. I have to get back to my family. We Mexican jays, you know, live in flocks, and we work together to fight off our enemies. I really must be off; my family needs me."

"Wait!" cried the ocotillo. "What about the baby? We have to help it."

"I'll find its mother," said the jay, "and I'll tell her where her baby is, but it won't do any good. It's far too cold; she won't be able to get here before the baby dies."

"No, no," said the ocotillo. "I'll keep the baby warm until its mother comes."

Promising that it would find the mother porcupine, the jay flew off toward the mountains.

The ocotillo spoke to the baby, which was shivering and crying softly. "Don't be afraid, little one. Everything will be all right."

The ocotillo bent over, scooped up some pine needles with its branches, and made a bed for the baby. Then it stretched one of its branches over to the live coal, and the branch caught on fire. Soon all the branches caught on fire, and they burned for a very long time. The baby porcupine stopped shivering in the warmth provided by the bush, but it did not cease to whimper and be frightened, for its mother was not there.

Just as the flames were dying, the mother porcupine came running up. Actually, she came waddling up, because that's what porcupines do. But she was waddling very fast!

The mother porcupine immediately went to her baby, cuddled it, and whispered to it. She felt a deep sense of relief when it whispered back to her. Only when she was certain that her baby was not harmed did she turn her attention to the ocotillo. Before her stood a bush whose branches were now the color of ash.

"Oh, my!" she gasped. "You look so exposed, so helpless! Let me give you some of my spines. We porcupines use them for protection." The mother porcupine put as many of her spines as she could spare all over the ocotillo's branches. Then she profusely thanked the ocotillo for what it had done and left with her baby.

Today, when the rains bring those small leaves to the ocotillo, there are no more bald spots. Although insects and lizards eat some of the leaves, most of the animals are wary of those spines and keep their distance.

Desert rains are infrequent however, and for most of the year the ocotillo looks like a bundle of gray, spiny, dead sticks.

But there is a time when the ocotillo is the grandest of all the desert bushes! In the spring, its branches are crowned with flowers in the shape and color of burning flames. In this way the Creator celebrates the compassion of the ocotillo, which gave up its beautiful turquoise branches when it set itself on fire to save a baby.

THE DEER BROTHERS

Even when circumstances drastically change,
the power of love remains binding.

One winter night, long ago, there was a strange but beautiful display in the sky above the mountains that are now called the White Tanks. It seemed as though the Creator had flung burning coals across the sky, coals that showered the sky with embers as they flew through the darkness.

Down in the valley, two brothers decided that they wanted to see this marvel more closely. They went to the mountains and climbed up to the top of the tallest one. There they found two plants, each a slight stalk with spines. Surrounding them was a small group of male deer. The bucks, or stags, were brown in color and had very large ears. Today we know these animals as mule deer.

A soft, ashen dust began to drift down from the sky. When it fell on the deer, they ran away, but not before the ashen dust changed the color of their coats to a grayish-brown. The brothers remained on the mountain top, and they experienced a change, too. They were turned into wild deer.

One might think that they were horrified, but no! They were pleased with their grayish-brown coats that looked silver on the mountain that night. They liked being able to turn their ears in any direction, without having to move their heads, and hearing sounds that they had never been able to hear before. They were delighted that they could take bounding leaps covering more than twenty feet and then come down stiffly on all fours, instantly change direction, and leap again.

After several days, when the brothers didn't come home, their worried parents went to the elders. "Did your sons go up into the mountains that night when the sky was on fire?" they asked the parents.

"Yes, yes, they did," the mother and father replied.

"Then they are lost to you," the elders told them, "because they were there when the boundaries in nature were blurred. We cannot say exactly what happened to your sons, but you must accept that they will not come back to you."

Indeed, the brothers did not return.

With the arrival of spring and longer days, they began to grow antlers, like the other male deer. At the same time, the two plants on the mountain top began to grow branches that looked very much like the antlers of the deer. Today, we call one of the plants the buckhorn cactus, and the other we know as the staghorn cactus. Like brothers, they are similar to each other, and they can be difficult to tell apart.

The brothers did not think about their parents and their sister, for they were now wild deer. Although the parents grieved for their sons, they had suffered loss before and understood that they had no choice but to accept this one. For their young daughter, however, it was a different matter. She could not accept it.

Finally, she went to her parents. "Mother, Father," she said, "I have to go look for my brothers; I must know what happened to them." Her parents tried to dissuade her, but they could not. There was nothing to do but give her their blessing and let her go.

She went up into the mountains, and when evening came, she found herself in the very spot at the top of the mountain where her brothers had been on that night when silver dust floated down from the sky.

When she saw the two plants with their unusual branches resembling deer antlers, she was amazed. "There are no plants like these anywhere else," she thought. "This has to be a special, magical place. I'll stay here, and surely something wondrous will happen." She sat down between the buckhorn and the staghorn cactus, and she quietly waited.

Her patience was rewarded. In the light of the moon, she could see two deer approach; they were magnificent with their antlers. They stood at a distance, but they never took their eyes off the young girl.

She tried to remain still and not do anything that would scare them away. Then, out of the corner of her eye, she caught sight of an animal creeping toward her from among the rocks. It was a mountain lion! She could not help but cry out from fright.

The two deer did not leave, however. Instead, they attacked the mountain lion, kicking it and jabbing it so fiercely with their antlers that it ran off. "They must be my brothers!" the girl thought. She knew that female deer, the does, would defend their young, even fawns that were not their own, yet these were male deer, and they had protected her, a human child!

For the rest of the night, the two deer watched over her. When morning came, they disappeared down the mountain.

The sister returned to her parents. "I have seen my brothers," she said. "The elders are right. They are lost to us, for they are now wild animals."

The family took comfort in the measure of love that had remained with the brothers and had guided them to shield the young girl. Did that love gradually fade away? There was no way to know: the brothers were never seen again. The parents and their daughter, however, held the wild deer brothers close to their hearts for the rest of their days.

How the Coyote Hurt the Moon

*The consequences of a selfish, foolish action can
break even the strong ties of friendship.*

Long ago, as the white moon drew her arc across the night sky, she looked down and saw something that was very curious. There seemed to be a white ribbon curving through some dark mountains. She decided to investigate. She came down from the sky and found herself in what today are called the White Tank Mountains of the Sonoran Desert.

The white ribbon turned out to be a desert wash where the water, when it flowed, wore off the dark outer layer covering the mountains, the layer called "desert varnish." Without that layer, the true white of the granite rocks was revealed.

The moon was quite taken with all the different kinds of plants and animals that she saw in the White Tanks, and one animal in particular—the coyote—was quite taken with her. The two became close friends.

Night after night, as the moon passed over the Sonoran Desert, she would take a break and come down to the White Tank Mountains. She and the coyote would dance together, the moon softly floating right above the ground, gracefully turning this way and that, and the coyote turning somersaults and kicking up his heels.

One night, the coyote stood upright and waved his front paws—in perfect rhythm because the coyote was a good dancer! The moon delicately blew on his underside, and the fur on the coyote's chest, underbelly, and inner legs turned white. The coyote felt very special!

A few nights later, as the moon floated over a saguaro, she ever so gently kissed the top of the cactus, and on that spot a white flower burst into bloom. Then she saw a rabbit, and she lightly touched his puffy tail. Instantly, the rabbit's tail was pure white.

"Look at the beautiful flower on the saguaro!" the animals exclaimed. Indeed, it was beautiful—so much so that today it is the state flower of Arizona. "And the rabbit's tail!" they cried. "It looks like a little ball of cotton." They were right. Today that rabbit is called the desert cottontail.

All the animals were thrilled by the moon's magic—all of them except for the coyote, that is. He wanted the moon to pay attention only to him. When the moon left that night to return to her place in the sky, the coyote sulked and didn't even tell her goodbye, as he usually did, and wish her "Bon voyage!"

The next day, the coyote was still angry. As he was trotting by the side of the desert wash, a little lizard darted out in front of him. "Get out of my way," the coyote snarled, batting the lizard aside.

The lizard hit his head on a rock, and the blow knocked him out. The animals gathered around in concern. "What happened?" they asked. When the lizard came to, however, he was confused and couldn't remember anything.

"Well, it had to be the moon's doing," said the coyote. "You know how clumsy she is."

That night, when the moon came down for her usual visit, the animals ganged up on her. "Watch out where you're going from now on! The coyote told us what you did."

The moon was bewildered. "What do you mean?" she asked.

"You barreled over a lizard and knocked him out. We were afraid that he was dead."

"But I'm always very careful," the moon said. "I'm sure I haven't hurt any of you."

Unfortunately, the animals wouldn't listen. "You think that you can just go wherever and do whatever you want. You think only about yourself." They kept on shouting at the moon, and the more they shouted, the meaner and crueler their words became.

Finally, the moon realized that it wasn't possible for her to convince the animals that she had done nothing wrong. Sadly she took her leave. The next night, she did not come down to the desert, nor did she come down the nights after that.

The coyote's anger turned to grief and guilt when he realized that he had lost her. He has those feelings to this very day. He can often be heard at night, calling to the moon and pleading with her to come back. The moon, however, has never returned.

Today, especially when the moon is full, one can see just how much the coyote and the other animals hurt her. For still today, her bruises are visible. Perhaps there are some injuries, those caused by words of unkindness and injustice, which never really go away.

The Bobcat and the Saguaro

*The power of love to unite is indisputable, but
what happens if the love is not returned?*

Long ago in the Sonoran Desert, a bobcat fell madly in love with a saguaro cactus. She was tall and stately, and the bobcat believed that she was the most beautiful being that ever there was. The saguaro was flattered by his attention.

Of course, lots of animals paid her attention. For example, the Gila woodpecker hollowed out holes for nests in her side. When the woodpecker abandoned the nest, the elf owl often moved in. For many animals the saguaro was a source of food, and bats, bees, and butterflies drank the nectar of her flowers.

The bobcat, on the other hand, wanted nothing from her but her affection.

He climbed forty feet up to the top of the saguaro and sat there for several days and nights. Before long, that situation became quite tiresome for the saguaro. The bobcat threatened other animals that came near, and since they were afraid of him, they stayed away. The saguaro found that she missed her friends and all their activity. It was boring to spend all her time with no one but the bobcat!

The saguaro tried to convey to him that the situation was not acceptable. "Please don't chase my friends away," she said more than once; "I like having them here." The bobcat refused to take her seriously, however, and there was no way she could force him to do as she requested. "Don't you want to spend some time somewhere else?" she asked several times, but the bobcat purringly responded that if she couldn't go with him, he wouldn't go either. He seemed unable to understand or accept that the saguaro did not share his feelings.

Finally, however, the bobcat's desire for togetherness was temporarily overcome by the growling in his empty stomach. He had to go find some food, so he climbed down, stood before the saguaro, and recited the following lines:

I must leave you, my dear, sweet Saguaro,
And my heart fills with torment and sorrow.
But, no tears, for I'll be back tomorrow.

"Oh, my," thought the saguaro. "Does he think that's poetry? It's awful! I can't stand this any longer!" While the bobcat was gone, the saguaro thought of how she could convince him to go on his way.

The next day, the bobcat returned and climbed up to the top of the saguaro, where he resumed extolling her beauty and claiming his undying love.

"You know," said the saguaro, "yesterday, while you were gone, I saw a bobcat..."

"What?" cried her unwelcome guest. "I'll tear him apart."

"No, no!" the saguaro said. "It was a she, not a he, bobcat, and she was something else! Her short little tail was most winsome, her whiskers were curly, and she had a 'come hither' look in her eyes. Oh, I'm sure you'd like her."

"Dearest Saguaro, how can you suggest such a thing?" said the bobcat. "You know that I am yours forever." And with that, he recited more of his "poetry."

You've won my heart,
I can't depart,
You are my star, O
Stout Saguaro!

"Stout?" said the saguaro. "Stout? Are you saying that I'm overweight?"

"Oh, my love," answered the bobcat. "You are so funny! Your sense of humor is another one of your endearing traits. You know that when I call you 'stout,' I'm saying that you are 'brave' and 'strong.'"

"I knew that! I knew that!" said the saguaro hastily. "But, really. I don't feel right about your interest in me. You should be with someone else, someone more sophisticated than I, someone who can truly appreciate your rare talents."

The bobcat laughed. "Dearest Saguaro, what a jokester you are!"

The next time the bobcat left to find something to eat, the saguaro called out to the animals. "Isn't there anything you can do to help me?"

"I'd slink up there and bite him," said the rattlesnake, "but I'm terrified of heights!"

The Anna's hummingbird, the Gila woodpecker, the elf owl, and many other birds all wanted to help, but they couldn't safely get close enough to the bobcat to do anything that would be effective.

But there was one bird that could help....

When the bobcat returned to the top of the saguaro, his declarations of everlasting love were interrupted by the sound of wings flapping—large wings! It was the Harris hawk, coming to the rescue. He felt sorry for the saguaro, and, moreover, he didn't like the idea of the bobcat's sitting on top of her. Sometimes he himself liked to use the top of the saguaro as an observation post.

The hawk flew over the bobcat, his talons wrapped around a rock. "What are you doing here with my girlfriend?" the hawk called out in his most intimidating way. Then, flying up into the sky, he dropped the rock. He didn't want to hurt the bobcat, but he did drop the rock with such precision that the bobcat heard it whistling right by his left ear. Then the hawk flew off to secure another rock and let it fall right by the bobcat's right ear.

Two such close calls caused the bobcat to lose his balance and fall all the way to the ground.

"I think you'd better leave," the saguaro sweetly suggested.

The bobcat didn't need to be told twice; that forty-foot fall from the top of the saguaro had plumb knocked the love out of him. He ran away as fast as he could, with the hawk's admonition—"And don't come back!"—ringing in his ears.

Since then, bobcats haven't displayed any interest in saguaros, and you may think that this story could never have happened. But you would be wrong!

The Cloud People Come to the Sonoran Desert

Compassion leaves its mark not only on those to whom it is shown, but on those who show it as well.

When we look at clouds, we often fancy that we see the shapes of people. When the world was truly young, however, the people that were seen in the clouds weren't mere shapes or images; they were real beings. They were the Cloud People.

Late one afternoon, the wind gently blew some of them down onto the Sonoran Desert. Their presence was a cause of concern to the animals, who were not used to seeing clouds down on their level, and they cautiously peered at the Cloud People from various places of safety such as holes, burrows, and caves.

Among the Cloud People in the desert that day was a little Cloud Girl. As she looked around at the larger, puffy clouds that she had come down to the desert with, she was startled to realize that they were all strangers to her. She knew that the Cloud People constantly faced the possibility of change. They might be gently floating together as a group when a sudden gust of wind would push them apart. "That must be what happened," she thought. "I've been separated from my friends!"

She made her way over to the middle of the Cloud People so that she could feel more secure and maybe even find someone small, like her, to play with. All of the Cloud People there that day, however, were on the order of young adults. They knew far more than she did about the transformations that Cloud People could undergo. They knew that not only could the wind separate them from each other, but it could alter them in shape, and sometimes they could be changed into fog or mist with no shape at all. They could even become something else entirely—dew, or rain, or snow, or hail. So these young Cloud People believed that it was important to live to the fullest whatever experience came their way. To celebrate their first and quite possibly last visit to the Sonoran Desert, they decided to have a formal ball.

It was spring in the Sonoran Desert, and the cacti were in bloom. Astounded at the beauty and many colors of the flowers, the Cloud People agreed that each of them would embrace a different cactus and absorb the color of its blossoms. What a vibrant affair this ball would be!

"A ball! How exciting!" exclaimed the little Cloud Girl. "I've never been to one. I can't wait!"

Unfortunately, the Cloud People were too busy planning their gala celebration to be interested in the little Cloud Girl. "Please don't get in our way," they said to her. "Just scuttle along and find something to do somewhere else."

Very disappointed, the little Cloud Girl left the excitement and the plan-making behind. She found a rock to sit on. Her head drooped down, and she fought back tears.

What a heartbreaking sight she was! All the animals felt sorry for her, but only three of them dared to venture out of their hiding places: a rattlesnake, a Gila monster, and a tarantula. The three animals made their way over to the little Cloud Girl.

"Please don't be sad," they said.

"I so wanted to go to the ball," sniffed the Cloud Girl. "But I was told to scuttle along!"

"Then let's just have our own ball here," the animals said. "What do we need to do?"

"I'm not really sure," answered the Cloud Girl. "But it involves dressing up in some way. The older ones are planning to use the colors of the cactus flowers. I don't think there will be any flowers left for me to use."

"You are just fine with your white," her new friends said to her. "Look at that saguaro with its white blossoms. They are just as beautiful as any of the colored ones."

The Cloud Girl had to agree. So her dress would remain white.

"But I need something more," she said. "I need some accessories!"

"If I wrap myself around your neck," said the rattlesnake, "I could be your necklace."

"That's a wonderful idea," said the Cloud Girl. "You could be a diamond necklace!" When she picked up the rattlesnake, diamond-like markings suddenly appeared all down its back.

"Oh, my," said the rattlesnake; "I feel so classy!"

"If I hold on to my tail," said the Gila monster, "you could carry me as a purse."

"Splendid," said the Cloud Girl. "You could be my beaded purse." When she picked up the Gila monster, its smooth body was instantly covered with little bumps, like beads.

"Look how stylish I am!" cried the Gila monster.

It was the tarantula's turn. "I could be your pin, or brooch," it suggested.

"Fabulous!" replied the Cloud Girl. "A gold pin would be perfect."

But when the Cloud Girl picked it up, it changed not into a golden, but rather into a light tannish, or blonde, color. "Oh, I like this," said the tarantula. "Don't change a thing! I want to be a blonde!"

So it was that the little Cloud Girl and her new friends had their own party.

Just as the sun was beginning to set, the wind picked up. The rattlesnake, Gila monster, and tarantula were left behind as all the Cloud People were carried on the breeze back up to the sky. What a sight it was! The animals couldn't believe their eyes. All the colors of the cactus flowers in the Sonoran Desert were now in the clouds that covered the sky. There was one little dot of white, but only the rattlesnake, Gila monster, and tarantula knew to look for it.

Today in the Sonoran Desert, the rattlesnake still has those diamond-shaped markings; we call the snake the western diamond-backed rattler. The Gila monster still has those bumps, or beads, all over its body. The tarantula is still so light in color that it is often called the blonde tarantula. Moreover, to this very day, all over the world, if there are clouds in the sky as the sun is setting, we can see in them every shade of yellow, orange, pink, red, and purple—and sometimes a small dot of white--thanks to the cactus blossoms of the Sonoran Desert.

The Palo Verde Tree and the Golden-Winged Creatures

Fulfillment may come in the act of emptying oneself.

Long ago in the land now called Arizona, there stood a palo verde tree. At that time, the palo verde was not like one today; at that time the tree was covered with large green leaves that were as soft as velvet. There was nothing, or no one, to enjoy its leaves, however, for the palo verde was totally alone. If ever any people or animals somehow, by accident, came around, they wasted no time leaving, for none of them wanted to be in this desolate spot where there was nothing but sand, rocks, and one lone tree. The palo verde was not bitter and bore its solitude with grace. It believed that surely the Creator, the Great Mystery Power, had put it there, in that forlorn spot, for a reason.

One day, it observed in the distance a very strange sight. It seemed as though coming toward it was a fleet of little boats, skimming across the surface of a sea of sand. As they moved closer, the palo verde realized that they were unlike anything that it had ever seen or heard about during the rare, short visits that it was paid. They were small winged creatures, with forewings and hind wings much like a butterfly but with a curling segmented tail and stinger like a scorpion. Whatever these strange creatures were, they were beautiful, for they were golden in color, and their wings were like mirrors made of golden glass.

The palo verde watched in amazement as the creatures came closer and closer. Finally, they were at the foot of the tree, taking refuge in the shade cast by its velvety green leaves.

The one that had led the others spoke first. "We greet you, Palo Verde Tree. Long have we been seeking you."

The palo verde wasn't sure that it had heard correctly. "Seeking me?" it thought. "I've never been sought out!"

The palo verde greeted the creatures in return. "You are welcome here," it said. "But where are you from? Why did you leave your home?"

In spite of their obvious weariness, the creatures patiently explained.

"We are from a land that lies far behind us. There were many animals there, and there were many people, too. We lived in harmony with the animals, for they respected the order intended by the Great Mystery Power. But there was only discord between us and the people."

"Why was that so?" asked the palo verde.

"At first, our golden glass wings drew them to us like a magnet. They were even ready to risk our sting just to capture us. They kept us in cages so as to admire us, and then they began to tear off our mirror-wings to use as ornaments for their clothing and their bodies."

A shudder ran through the entire gathering of creatures as they remembered these things. And the palo verde shuddered, too.

"That was bad enough, Palo Verde Tree. But then they realized that what they saw when they looked into our mirror-wings was not the reflection of who they were, but of who they should be. Although each person was quick to admit the shortcomings of others, no one wanted to face the reality of his or her own imperfections. The people began to hunt us down, day and night, in order to kill us all. We had no choice but to leave."

All the creatures murmured in agreement. The palo verde murmured also.

"We had heard that at the half-way point in our long and difficult journey, we would find a tree, all by itself. You are that tree, Palo Verde, and it is our prayer that you will help us."

"Of course," the tree responded. "Just tell me what it is that you need."

"Kind Palo Verde Tree, the song that the Great Mystery Power gave us to sing in this world is but a few notes from ending, and we are the last of our kind. But if you would allow our females to lay eggs among your branches, then our species could continue. The young could feed on your leaves until they were strong enough to leave for their destination, a land that lies far ahead."

The palo verde tree hesitated for only a split second. It did not tell the creatures what would happen if it lost its velvety green leaves.

"Yes, of course, the females may lay their eggs in my branches. And your young would be welcome to stay here with me."

The creatures explained that, no, the young could not remain.

"The time is coming, Palo Verde Tree, when you will not be alone, when many of the animals and the people who dwell in the land behind us will come here to live. Our kind must be far away, for our golden mirror-wings, though a blessing, are also a curse to us."

And so it was that the females laid their eggs in the palo verde tree, and then they and the male creatures slowly and with great dignity flew away to meet their end.

The eggs hatched, and the young creatures ate their fill of the palo verde's large leaves. Every day they thanked it for sharing its leaves with them. They did not know what this generosity would cost the tree, and the palo verde did not tell them. The time came when the creatures left and continued the journey of those who had gone before them. The palo verde tree watched until their golden mirror-wings no longer glinted in the sun.

The branches of the palo verde were now completely bare.

In time, leaves grew back, but they were not the large, dark green velvet leaves the tree had before. The leaves grew out on thin little stems in pairs, and they were very small. The palo verde's leaves are still that way today.

There are those now who say that the palo verde is a sad looking tree that resembles a bony, ragged street urchin. Others disagree, finding the palo verde to be like a young girl at the first blush of maturity, dressed in fine green lace.

No matter how one sees the leaves of the palo verde, however, there comes the time, once a year, when everyone agrees that the tree is stunningly beautiful, like a bride carrying her wedding bouquet spray. For every spring the Great Mystery Power completely fills the branches of the tree with radiant yellow blossoms, as bright as the sun. These flowers honor the palo verde's sacrifice to save the exquisite golden creatures that left the land we call Arizona and dwell we know not where.

Perhaps someday, when we have learned to be the people we should be, the creatures will return!

WHAT THE IRONWOOD TREE
LEARNED FROM THE JAVELINA

*It is acceptance with the heart, not understanding with
the mind, that leads to being at one with the world.*

Long ago in the Sonoran Desert, there was a young ironwood tree that was deeply saddened by what took place around it. It was witness to flash floods that carried both plants and animals away in a sudden rush of water. It stood through storms with strong winds that toppled other trees and with lightning bolts that struck tall saguaros, causing them to burst open. Moreover, every day, without fail, the ironwood saw how the animals not only helped themselves to the flowers, seeds, and leaves of plants but hunted and preyed on each other as well.

The ironwood was so disheartened that it refused to take part in the world around it. It discouraged any plants or animals from coming near it, and after a while, none of them even wanted to be anywhere close. Ultimately, the ironwood's sadness and solitude had their effect on the tree itself. First, the wood of the tree became so hard and heavy that it would not float, and still today, if a piece of ironwood falls into water, it sinks to the bottom like a rock. In addition, the flowers of the tree became such a deep purple that they looked almost black.

Once, when the sky was filled with the soft light that follows the setting of the sun, a small group of javelinas came into the area where the ironwood stood. Like javelinas today, they could not see well, and the oldest among them had the weakest vision of all. Nonetheless, it could see what was hidden from most. It had insight into the inner nature of things, and it immediately sensed the suffering of the ironwood with its dark purple flowers.

The old javelina greeted the tree in its friendliest voice.

The ironwood was not at all responsive, but the javelina persisted. "Good evening," it said again.

"I wouldn't call the evening good," replied the ironwood. "I wouldn't call any part of the day or night 'good.' Why would it be, when life here means nothing; it is nothing but loss."

At the urging of the uninvited visitor to explain why it held such a bleak view of life, the ironwood told the javelina of the events it had witnessed that day alone, events that it found too pitiless to bear. When it had finished, it said, "The world makes no sense. It is too full of pain, and I won't be a part of it."

"What a sensitive sort you are!" said the javelina. "And that is good, for that means that you are caring and kind. But your thoughts have tortured you and led you to despair."

The ironwood remained silent.

"And that is good, too," continued the javelina. "Do you know why? Your despair reveals your realization that you are not, and cannot be, the boss in charge of everything. Now that humility has seeped into your very core, you can find true happiness."

"For pity's sake, what are you babbling about?" the ironwood responded. "You don't have any wisdom to pass on to me. You're just like the rest. You eat plants, and you eat animals, too."

"It's true that I do. In turn, I have also lost my young to other animals. But don't be too quick to judge me. Do you really think that you and the other plants don't take advantage of the world around you? When the rain falls, you drink its water. When the sun shines, you absorb its light. And the rain and the sun don't say, 'There go those greedy plants, exploiting us again. Let's go off somewhere else and leave them on their own.'

"You see, dear friend, everything is connected. And when we feel our connection to others, when we act for and with them, we can come to love the world, every part of it. That kind of love is the most difficult love of all. It is life's greatest achievement."

The ironwood still remained silent. The javelina saw that its group was moving to another spot, so it said goodbye to the tree and went on its way.

"Good riddance!" thought the ironwood. "What nonsense!"

But as the days went by, it found itself reflecting on what the javelina had said. It thought about the fact that every day, no matter what, the crickets and the cicadas filled the air with a chorus that celebrated the unfolding of life.

After a while, the ironwood missed the presence of the javelina, and it realized just how lonely it had become. It began calling out to the plants and animals, "Come on over; you're welcome here."

At first, it was the plants that took the ironwood up on its invitation. A young saguaro and a night-blooming cereus, for example, were delighted to find that the ironwood tree would provide them with shade from the sun and with protection from the frost as well.

Then various animals began to investigate the ironwood's offer of hospitality. "You'll find my roots offer lots of places to burrow," the ironwood told the tortoise. "My branches would make good roosting and nesting sites for you," it suggested to the hawk, the owl, and the dove. "My leaves are especially tasty," the ironwood told the pronghorn, the bighorn sheep, and the antelope. "You'll like my seeds," it said to the mice, squirrels, and quail. "The nectar in my flowers is especially sweet!" it told the bees.

Today, because of the support that the ironwood gives to so many plants and animals, it is known as a "nurse plant," and it is one of the most vital plants in the Sonoran Desert. Moreover, through its many ties to life forms in the desert, it has achieved that love that the javelina spoke of, that is, a love that embraces the whole of the world. Such a love often brings with it the gift of tears, and so it is with the ironwood. It weeps with both sorrow and joy at the mystery of creation, and its tears stain and wash out the dark purple of its petals. That is why today, when spring comes, the Sonoran Desert is filled with the soft lavender flowers of the ironwood tree.

Joyce Story

Joyce has been an Arizona resident for over thirty years and a storyteller for much of that time. This collection of her folkloric tales about the plants and animals of the Sonoran Desert is a natural outcome of her love for the desert and of her esteem for the imaginative tales of nature found in oral traditions throughout the world. She has also responded as an author and storyteller to the real-life experiences of family and friends in Florida, the state where she was born and raised; her collection of narrative poems entitled *The Rhyme and Rhythm of Childhood* was inspired by memories she heard from relatives and friends as she was growing up.

Joyce has formally studied Romance languages and literatures and holds a Ph.D. in Slavic languages and literatures. She is a retired college educator in the fields of her academic training and in the art of storytelling as well.

Appreciation

Grateful acknowledgement is made to Jim Poulter for his kind permission to adapt his work "The Secret of Dreaming."
http://www.jimpoulter.com/secretofdreaming.html

Resources for Photographs

The Secret of Dreaming
1. Alesandra Blakeston
   http://about.me/alesandra
   http://alesandrab.wordpress.com/tag/shapes/
   http://www.pifsc.noaa.gov/qrb/2012_10/article_17.php
2. Jerrye And Roy Klotz MD
   http://commons.wikimedia.org/wiki/File%3ALONG_NOSED_LEOPAR D_LIZARD_-_DEATH_VALLEY%2C_CA.jpg
3. Joseph R. Tomelleri
   http://www.fishesoftexas.org/taxon/agosia-chrysogaster
4. Rene Mensen
   http://commons.wikimedia.org/wiki/File:Jaguar_(4064767455).jpg
5. The National Oceanic and Atmospheric Administration
   Tropical Depression Seventeen-W on August 14, 1996
   http://lwf.ncdc.noaa.gov/oa/ncdc.html Land and ocean data
   http://visibleearth.nasa.gov/view_set.php?categoryID=2355

The Desert Tortoise and the Free-tailed Bat
1. http://www.keepbanderabeautiful.org/mob-bats.html
2. Paul Condon
   http://www.azgfd.gov/w_c/tortoiseencounter.shtml

The Birds Petition the Creator
1. Steve Berardi
   http://steveberardi.com/NASA-
   http://www.nasa.gov/multimedia/imagegallery/image_feature_693.html

How the Mountain Lion Met His Match
1. Anna Magdalena Łysiak
   Anna MagdalenaŁysiak
   http://commons.wikimedia.org/wiki/File:Mountain_lion_in_Albright_Vi sitor_Center,_museum_-_Fort_Yellowstone.JPG
2. Gracey Stinson
   gracey.stinson@gmail.com
   http://morguefile.com/archive/display/27647

Return of the Night Sky
1. Michael Hartl
   Weaver spider web at night |Source=Own work |Date=2004-09-11
   Permission=Public domain

2. http://www.bugbusters.com/spiders.html

Larcena Page and the Beyond World
1. http://www.cinemaartscentre.org

How the Ocotillo Saved a Baby
1. http://26.media.tumblr.com/tumblr_lv0ae6WPjk1qlme4do1_500.jpg

Deer Brothers
1. Brent Stettler
   Utah Division of Wildlife Resources
   http://www.xploreutah.net/story/apply-big-game-permit-starting-friday#gallery-jump
2. Franck Rolland
   Buckhorn cholla - Opuntia acanthocarpa @ Organ Pipe Cactus NM – AZ
   http://commons.wikimedia.org/wiki/File:Buckhorn_Cholla.JPG
3. NASA/JPL-Caltech/UCLA
   http://www.nasa.gov/multimedia/imagegallery
4. Owen Borseth
   owen@borseth.us
   https://plus.google.com/100722414482526781723/posts

The Bobcat and the Saguaro
1. Curt Fonger
   curtfonger@msn.com
   http://www.visionsofthesw.com/

The Cloud People Come to the Sonoran Desert
1. Gayle Lindgren
   gayle.lindgren@yahoo.com;
   Desert Sunset Phoenix Arizona #Image ID: 1266452
2. J. Durham
   http://www.morguefile.com/archive/display/524332
3. Xandert
   http://www.morguefile.com/creative/xandert

20133204R00049

Made in the USA
San Bernardino, CA
29 March 2015